P9-DGD-447

Text © 2001 by Chronicle Books.
Illustrations © 2001 by Julie Paschkis.
All rights reserved.

Book design by Alethea Morrison. Typeset in Adobe Garamond.
The illustrations in this book were rendered in gouache.
Printed in China.

Library of Congress Cataloging-in-Publication Data
Paschkis, Julie.
    The nutcracker / illustrated by Julie Paschkis.
p. cm.
Summary: A young girl receives a nutcracker for Christmas and, after learning how he
got his ugly face, helps break a spell and change him into a handsome prince.
    ISBN 0-8118-2962-6
    [1. Fairy tales. 2. Christmas—Fiction.] I. Hoffmann, E. T. A.
(Ernst Theodor Amadeus), 1776–1822. Nußknacker und Mäusekönig. II.
Title.
PZ8.P26 Nu 2001
[Fic]--dc21
    00-011734

Distributed in Canada by Raincoast Books
9050 Shaughnessy Street, Vancouver, British Columbia V6P 6E5

10 9 8 7 6 5 4 3 2 1

Chronicle Books LLC
85 Second Street
San Francisco, California 94105
www.chroniclebooks.com/Kids

THE NUTCRACKER

BASED ON THE CLASSIC STORY BY E. T. A. HOFFMANN

ILLUSTRATED BY JULIE PASCHKIS

chronicle books · san francisco

MUSICAL SELECTIONS

Following are the musical selections from *The Nutcracker* by Tchaikovsky that are included on the enclosed compact disc.

ACT 1

1 *Overture*

2 *The Christmas Tree*

3 *March*

4 *Journey Through the Snow*

5 *Waltz of the Snowflakes*

ACT 2

6 *Le Chocolat (Spanish Dance)*

7 *Le Café (Arabian Dance)*

8 *Le Tea (Chinese Dance)*

9 *Trepak (Russian Dance)*

10 *Dance of the Mirlitons*

11 *Mother Gigogne & the Clowns*

12 *Waltz of the Flowers*

13 *Paux de Deux*

14 *Tarentella*

15 *Dance of the Sugar-Plum Fairy*

16 *Coda*

17 *Final Waltz & Apotheose*

All tracks performed by the London Symphony Orchestra, Don Jackson, Conductor. All tracks produced by Paul Whitehead for Iliad, Inc. Recorded at the C-T-S Studios, Wembley, England, by David Hunt and remixed at the Iliad Studios in Nashville by Hollis Halford. ℗1994 Iliad, Inc. Courtesy of Iliad, Inc. Manufactured by BMG Special Products, a unit of BMG Entertainment.

INTRODUCTION

The Nutcracker ballet has become a cherished part of the Christmas tradition. Each year there are more than one thousand productions of the ballet performed around the world, with audiences numbering in the millions. But what many people don't know is that the ballet is derived from a story written nearly one hundred years before the ballet debuted.

That story was written by E. T. A. Hoffmann, a lawyer who turned to music and writing after Napoleon invaded his native Prussia in 1806. In 1815, Hoffmann encountered his first nutcracker in the Leipzig market, and in 1816, he wrote a tale called *The Nutcracker and the Mouse King.*

In 1891, the director of the Imperial Theater in St. Petersburg decided to create a ballet based on the story, and he approached Peter Ilyich Tchaikovsky to create the musical score. However, in order to better showcase the dancers, the ballet was based on a sweeter version of the tale, which had been written in 1844 by French author Alexander Dumas, *pere.* This new version eliminated much of the darkness of Hoffmann's original. Likewise, it greatly expanded Clara's (in some versions also known as Marie) visit to the Land of Sweets. The ballet debuted in December 1892 at the Mariinsky Theater, home of the Kirov Ballet. It was first performed outside Russia in 1934 and in the United States in 1940.

This very special edition combines a full-length music CD of Tchaikovsky's magnificent score with Hoffmann's original version of the story. This version includes Hoffmann's very important "Story of the Hard Nut," a story-within-the-story that was not included in the ballet. It is through this element that readers truly come to understand the wickedness of the Mouse King, the strength of the Nutcracker and the tender and brave loyalty of Clara, making *The Nutcracker* the quintessential holiday fairy tale.

Christmas Eve

It was Christmas Eve. The whole day through Clara and Fritz had not been allowed to go into the sitting room. Since early that morning they had heard knockings and people moving about. And not an hour ago, a man with a large box had gone past on tiptoe; but they knew who it was—it was their godfather, Uncle Drosselmeier.

Uncle Drosselmeier was small and thin, and his face was covered with little crisscross wrinkles, as if a spider had spun its web all over his skin. Over his right eye he wore a black patch. Uncle Drosselmeier was also very clever. He knew how to make clocks. Whenever one of the clocks in the house had something the matter with it, along came Uncle Drosselmeier, who took off his yellow coat, tied a blue apron round his waist, and commenced to poke about inside the clock.

Every time Uncle Drosselmeier visited he brought treats. And on Christmas he always brought a toy that he had made himself. Fritz thought that this time it must be a fort with fine soldiers. "No, no!" said Clara, "Uncle has been telling me all about a beautiful garden with a large lake and white swans with gold collars." The two children sat talking for some time, trying to guess what Uncle Drosselmeier had made and what there would be under the Christmas tree for them. Clara wanted a new parasol for her favorite doll. Fritz wanted soldiers on horseback.

When it was quite dark, they sat very close together, quietly listening. Suddenly a bright light shone under the door. Then a silver bell rang, *cling, cling! cling-a-ling!* The door flew open, and such a dazzling light shone into the room that both Clara and Fritz gasped and then stood quite still, looking and looking. It was a Christmas tree—far, *far* more beautiful than any they had ever seen.

The Christmas Presents

Fritz and Clara must have been very good children. Golden and silver apples, sugar cakes, chocolates, and other delicious treats hung from every branch. Hundreds of lights twinkled like stars. Under the tree there was a lovely silk doll dress for Clara. And for Fritz there were toy soldiers, dressed in scarlet and riding fine white horses.

The little bell rang again. It was time to see Uncle Drosselmeier's present. The cloth over it was slowly lifted, and before them stood a magnificent castle. *Ding, ring-a-ding!* The golden doors and crystal windows flew open, and out came a number of dainty gentlemen and ladies dressed in fine clothes and wearing hats with plumes. Inside the castle, which was lit by candles in silver candlesticks, tiny children danced. A gentleman no taller than Father's thumb and clad in a purple cloak looked out one of the windows, nodded his head twice, and then disappeared.

"Uncle Drosselmeier," Fritz said, "let me go into your castle." Uncle Drosselmeier told him that was impossible since it was not even as tall as Fritz himself. "Well, then, let the children come out. I want to look at them!" said Fritz. "It's no good asking for things like that," said Uncle Drosselmeier, in quite a cross voice. "I made it to work just as you see it now, and it won't work in any other way."

"Well," said Fritz, "if your little figures are always doing the same thing, and can't do anything else, I don't think I care about them very much. I like my soldiers far better." Then he ran away to play.

Clara had also crept quietly away. And while everyone else was merrily opening their gifts, she found something very interesting underneath the Christmas tree. There, behind Fritz's soldiers, was a little man. He was standing quite patiently, as if waiting for his turn.

Little Nutcracker

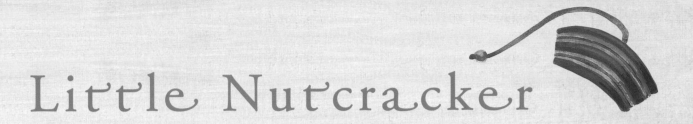

He certainly was not beautiful. His legs were short and his head very big. From his shoulders hung a stiff mantle. But he wore a handsome purple jacket and matching trousers. And through his beard of white cotton one could see his pleasant smile.

"Oh, Father!" cried Clara, "look at this dear little man!"

"It's a nutcracker," replied Father. He put a nut into its mouth, lifted up the wooden mantle and—*crack!*—the shell broke into pieces. Clara gave the nutcracker some more nuts. She carefully chose the smallest, so that he should not be obliged to open his mouth too wide. When Fritz heard the nuts being cracked, he came running. He pushed the largest nuts he could find into the nutcracker's mouth. Suddenly—*crack, crack! crack!*—three little teeth fell out of the nutcracker's mouth.

"Oh, my poor Nutcracker!" cried Clara, taking him away from Fritz. "You are a mean boy. Go away!"

"No, he belongs to me, too!" cried Fritz. "Give him back."

Clara began to cry. When Father heard what had happened, he said, "Now that he is hurt, nobody else but Clara shall look after him."

Fritz looked ashamed and went to find his soldiers. Clara tied up Nutcracker's chin in a piece of soft linen. Then she carefully wrapped Nutcracker in her handkerchief. Uncle Drosselmeier laughed and asked her why she took such great care of such an ugly fellow. "If you were dressed like dear Nutcracker, and had such beautiful shiny shoes," she said, "who knows whether you would look half as nice as he does!"

She did not understand why both Father and Mother laughed when she said this, and why Uncle Drosselmeier turned very red in the face and did not laugh at all.

A Strange Adventure

In the nursery was a large cupboard with glass doors. On the topmost shelf stood the toys that Uncle Drosselmeier had made. On the next shelf were picture books. Next, Fritz's soldiers. The bottom shelf was filled with Clara's dolls. There were several little chairs beside a tea table and a little bed for her favorite doll.

It was already quite late, but the children could not tear themselves away from the cupboard, although Mother kept saying, "It's time to go to bed, children!" over and over again.

"Yes, yes!" replied Fritz at last, "My poor soldiers are quite ready for bed, but so long as I am here they dare not close their eyes." He tidied them all up and went off to bed himself. But Clara begged, "Oh, Mother, let me stay here just a little while! Then I will go to bed, I promise!"

"For just a few minutes," said her mother. "But then it's time for bed."

Clara turned her attention again to the wounded Nutcracker. She laid him gently down and unwound the handkerchief. He smiled so sadly that Clara felt she could have cried.

"Oh, little Nutcracker!" she whispered, "I will take good care of you, and Uncle Drosselmeier shall put all your teeth back and mend your chin."

She could scarcely finish what she had to say, for at the name of Uncle Drosselmeier, Nutcracker twisted his face up in a curious way, and his eyes shone bright green. Clara felt quite frightened, but when she looked again she saw only the poor little fellow smiling sadly up at her as he had done before.

"How silly I am!" she thought. "Fancy believing that a toy could make faces!"

Clara laid Nutcracker down upon the doll's bed. Then she shut the cupboard and was going to leave the room when—hark!—she heard a gentle rustling, a creaking, a whispering! Up the chimney, behind the cupboard, up and down, all around her!

The big grandfather clock began to tick louder and louder—*tick, tock, TOCK, TICK!* Suddenly its round face lit up, then its body, and there inside stood Uncle Drosselmeier, with his coattails swinging to and fro like a pendulum—*pum, pum, pum, pum!*—and all the time he sang:

"**Pum,** *p u m,* **pum,** *p u m,* Do you hear the Mouse King come? up, up, down, down, *Mouse King* wears a golden crown. He is ready for the *F I G H T,* he can *scratch* and he can **B I T E!** **Pum,** *p u m,* **pum,** *p u m, RUSTLE, BUSTLE, Mouse King,* **C O M E!**"

Then the clock struck—*pum, pum, pom, pom!*—twelve times.

Clara was frightened. But before she could run away, there was such a whistling and squeaking all around her, such a trotting, such a scampering, such a running behind the walls of the room, as if a thousand little feet were pattering all at once, and a thousand little lights twinkled through the cracks.

The Battle

But they were not really lights! In another minute, *trot, trot, scamper, scamper!* troops of mice, in twos and threes, in threes and fours, came up through the floor, in through the walls, and arranged themselves just as Fritz's soldiers did before battle.

Right in front of Clara the floor cracked, and seven mouse heads with seven glittering crowns came up, the heads squeaking loudly. Next came the body to which the seven heads belonged—the Mouse King! He ran to the head of the army, and off went the mouse soldiers, *scamper, scamper!* toward the cupboard. Clara's heart was beating so fast that it seemed as if it might burst. She was just trying to move out of the way when, *crack, crack!* the glass doors of the cupboard fell in pieces! Clara felt a smarting pain in her arm.

But what was that noise? In the cupboard there was a whispering, and little voices began to sing: *"Wake, w a k e,* 'tis light, make ready for the *FIGHT! Wake, w a k e, PREPARE!* The *King of Mice* is there!"

Then the cupboard lit up, and there was such a rustle, a bustle, a marching, and a tramping as Clara had never heard before. The toys, dolls, soldiers were all alive! Suddenly Nutcracker arose and threw off the bedcover, crying out: *"Crack, crack, crack,* fall upon the *PACK. Crack, crack, crick,* fall upon them *QUICK!"*

Then he drew his little sword, and waving it in the air he shouted: "Dear friends, who is on my side?" All the toys, Teddy Bears, Gollywogs, and Jumping Jacks shouted: "We are!" and followed Nutcracker. "Drummer, sound the Advance!" he cried. The drum began to roll, *pom, pom, pompitty pom!* Regiment after regiment of toy soldiers came marching down with flags flying and music playing. In front of the army rolled the cannons. *Boom, boom!* they began to shoot sugar-plums at the mouse army.

The noise was tremendous, *pop, pop, pop! bang, bang, bang! boom, boom, boom!* The mice squeaked, and Nutcracker shouted commands at the top of his voice. The mice kept pushing nearer and nearer, then flung themselves upon Nutcracker's army. The toys began to retreat, leaving Nutcracker standing alone in front of the cupboard. Soon he was quite surrounded by the enemy and in the greatest danger, for the Mouse King, squeaking triumphantly, was about to pounce on him.

"Oh, my poor Nutcracker!" Clara cried. Before she knew what she was doing she had taken the shoe off her left foot and flung it, as hard as she could, right at the Mouse King.

Instantly the noise ceased, and Clara fell to the ground in a faint.

Clara's Dream

When Clara awoke she found herself in her bed. The sun was shining brightly through the window.
By her bedside sat her mother.

"Oh, Mother," said Clara, "have all the ugly mice gone, and was my dear Nutcracker saved after all?"

"What *are* you talking about, Clara?" asked Mother. "Oh, what a fright you have given us! You must
have fallen against the glass door of the cupboard, for you cut your arm very badly. I found you lying by the
cupboard, and all around you on the floor were scattered Fritz's soldiers. Nutcracker was close by your side,
and not far away was one of your shoes."

"That was because there was a great battle between the mice and the soldiers," said Clara. "I threw my shoe at the Mouse King to save my poor Nutcracker."

"There, there," said Mother. "The mice are all gone, and everything is safe back in the cupboard again."

Clara had to stay in bed all day and drink nasty medicine. At the end of the day Uncle Drosselmeier came to pay her a visit. "Well, well! How is the little patient?"

Clara cried out, "Oh, you mean Uncle! I saw you inside the clock! I heard you singing about the Mouse King! Why didn't you help Nutcracker? It's all your fault that I am lying in bed here!"

Uncle then sang in a high, piping voice: "**Pum,** *pum, Pendulum!* up and down and *round* the house runs the *NAUGHTY* little mouse. **Bim,** *bim, bim!* Do you see him? *Cling,* **clang!** *Clang,* **cling!** Yes, it is the *Mousey-King.* **Pick, pack,** *POCK!* Hearken to the *CLOCK!* **Boom!** *Bim!* **BOOM!**"

Clara looked at Uncle with wide-open eyes as he sang and swung his arm to and fro like a pendulum. Fritz, who had just come into the room, burst out laughing. Mother was quite vexed. "Why do you do that when you know that it will only make Clara ill again?"

"Dear me!" replied Uncle, with a laugh, "I sing that song when I am mending my clocks, and I thought Clara would like to hear it."

Then he sat down by Clara's bed and whispered, "You mustn't be angry with me." He put his hand in his pocket and drew out little Nutcracker, with all the lost teeth back in his mouth again.

Clara said with a smile, "How beautifully you have mended Nutcracker."

"Yes," said Uncle "but he's an ugly little fellow all the same. Do you know the story of why all the Nutcracker family is so ugly?"

"No, no!" cried Fritz. "Tell it to us."

"Well," said Uncle, "it begins like this."

The Story of the Hard Nut

Pirlipat was a princess, the most beautiful little girl anyone had ever seen. Her skin looked as if it were made out of roses, her eyes were as blue as the sky, and her hair was like gold. She had two rows of little teeth just like pearls, and when the King's Prime Minister bent down to look at her, she bit his finger so hard that he cried out, "Oh! oh! oh!"

The Princess's cradle was guarded by six nurses, each with a cat on her lap. All night long they stroked these cats, in order to make them purr. The reason they did so was this: One time Pirlipat's father invited to supper a great many kings and queens, princes and princesses. He asked the queen to prepare his favorite dish, bacon and sausages. But the moment the bacon began to sizzle, the Queen heard a little voice whispering, "Sister, sister, give me some of your bacon!"

The Queen knew at once that it was Mouseyrink. This mouse had lived for a great many years in the palace. She always said that she was related to the royal family and that she was queen in the kingdom of mice. Pirlipat's mother was a kind lady, and although she did not really think that Mouseyrink was a queen like herself, called out, "Come here, Mouseyrink! You can have some of my bacon."

Mouseyrink ran out of her hole and seized the pieces of bacon. The Mouse Queen's friends and relations came running too, and also her seven sons, who were very impudent mice. Luckily, the Royal Mistress of the Kitchen came in just at that moment and chased the uninvited guests away. A little bacon was still left, and this was carefully cut up into small pieces.

When the feast began, the King began to weep. "Too little bacon!" he sobbed. The Queen threw herself at his feet, "Oh, my! Mouseyrink and all her friends and relations have eaten up the bacon!" The King cried that he would be revenged. The Royal Clockmaker, whose name was Drosselmeier, was ordered to get rid of the mice. He made some traps in which a piece of bacon was hung upon a piece of string.

Now Mouseyrink was much too clever to be taken in by a trick like this, but in spite of all her warnings six of her seven sons, tempted by the delicious smell of the bacon, were caught. The whole Court rejoiced when they heard the news. But the Queen knew what a wicked creature Mouseyrink was, and knew that she would make them all suffer for the slaying of her sons.

Sure enough, one day Mouseyrink appeared and said, "Take care, O Queen, that I do not bite your little princess in two. Take care!" Then she disappeared again.

Here Uncle Drosselmeier stopped and said that they should hear the rest of the story tomorrow.

More About the Hard Nut

The next day Uncle Drosselmeier called the children together and continued his story:
Now you know why the Queen was so careful about watching her beautiful little daughter.
The Clockmaker's traps were no use at all; Mouseyrink would not
go near them. The Royal Stargazer said that Mouseyrink
could only be kept away from the princess by
cats, and so each of Pirlipat's nurses held a
purring cat on her lap.

One night the head nurse fell
asleep, then woke with a start. There
was not a sound to be heard; not a
single cat was purring. They were
all asleep! The nurse saw a great
big ugly mouse, standing on its
hind legs, its head upon the
face of the little Princess.

The nurse sprang up
with a cry of terror, and Mouseyrink—for it was she and no other
—quickly ran away, disappearing

through a hole in the floor. Pirlipat awoke with a cry. "Thank Heaven!" exclaimed the nurse, "she is alive!" But instead of the pretty face she saw a big ugly head; it sat atop a small crooked body and the mouth stretched from one ear to the other!

The Queen nearly died of grief when she saw what had happened. The King realized he should have left the Mouse Queen and her sons in peace, but instead blamed the Royal Clockmaker. He ordered Drosselmeier to change the Princess back into her proper shape within fourteen days or else have his head cut off.

Master Drosselmeier was, of course, greatly frightened when he heard this, but as he was a very clever clockmaker he set to work at once to see what he could do. He went to the Stargazer, and the two friends set to work to find something in the stars and magic books about enchanted princesses. After a great deal of trouble they found out that in order to free the Princess from her enchantment they had to give her the Crickcrack nut to eat, a nut with such a hard shell that a steamroller could go over it without cracking it. This hard nut had to be given to the Princess by a young man who had never worn boots. After he had cracked it himself he had to present it to the Princess with his eyes shut. Then he had to take seven steps backward without stumbling before opening his eyes again.

The Clockmaker rushed to tell the King that he had found a way to set the Princess free. The King embraced him and promised to give him a sword with a handle covered with diamonds, as well as a fine red coat. Master Drosselmeier did not know what to say when he heard this. At last, in fear and trembling, he told the King that although they knew how to set the Princess free, they had not yet found either the young man or the hard nut.

The King decreed that the Clockmaker must go away. If he was able to find the young man and the nut, he would be forgiven; until that happened he wished never to see his face again.

Why Nutcracker Is So Ugly

Master Drosselmeier went to visit to his brother, the Royal Toymaker. He told him the story of the Princess Pirlipat and the Mouse Queen, and all about the hard nut. The Toymaker cried out in astonishment, "Brother, I have that very nut in my house!" Then he drew a large nut out of a bag, and there, printed on the shell, was the word "Crickcrack"! You can imagine how glad the Clockmaker was when he saw this. "One piece of good luck follows another," he cried. "We have not only found the nut Crickcrack, but also the young man who is to crack it." And it was quite true, for the son of the Toymaker was a young man who had never worn boots!

When the King announced that the nut had been found, hundreds of people flocked to the palace to see if they could crack it. One after another they tried, but *crack, crack!* out fell their teeth, and each one sighed as he was carried away to the dentist, "Oh, that was a hard nut!" At last the King promised that any man who succeeded in cracking the nut should marry the Princess and receive half the kingdom as a reward.

At this, the Clockmaker's nephew stepped forward and asked to be allowed to try. Princess Pirlipat was quite delighted to see him. She said with a sigh, "Ah, if only he could be the one to crack the hard nut!" The nephew bowed very politely to the King and Queen, and then to the Princess, took the nut in his hand, put it between his teeth, pulled his pigtail, and, *crack!* the shell broke into pieces!

He then carefully removed the kernel, shut his eyes, handed it to the Princess, and began to take seven steps backward. The Princess swallowed the kernel, and before you could count to "one," in place of the ugly little wretch there stood a beautiful girl! All those around cried, "Hip, hip, hurrah!" The trumpeters blew their trumpets and the drummers beat their drums. The King and Queen danced about for joy.

The Clockmaker's nephew was just stretching out his foot to take the seventh step when suddenly out from a hole in the floor popped Mouseyrink. The young man trod right on her, and then—oh, dear!—his body shriveled up until it was so small that it could scarcely carry the big head with its wide-open mouth. Instead of his pigtail there hung down his back a small cloak made of wood. The Mouse Queen lay helpless on the floor. "**Crick,** *crick,* **CRACK!** You've broken my *BACK!* My son, the *King of Mice,* is coming in a trice, **BEWARE!** Take *CARE! Queek! queek!*" And that was the end of her.

The Princess remembered what the King had promised, and ordered the poor Clockmaker's nephew to be brought to her. But when he came forward, looking so very, *very* ugly and crooked and wooden, she cried, "Oh take him away! Take that dreadful Nutcracker away!" The King did not want a nutcracker for his daughter's husband. He declared that it was all the fault of the Clockmaker, and he ordered him to leave the palace forever.

Once again, the Clockmaker went to the Stargazer, who read the stars and found out that in spite of his ugly shape Nutcracker would in the end become a king. But—and you must be careful to remember this!—before he could be changed back again two things had to happen. First of all, Nutcracker must kill the only remaining son of the Mouse Queen, and secondly, a maiden, a princess or not, must love him, in spite of his ugly face.

"That, children," said Uncle Drosselmeier, "is the story of the hard nut. Now you know why people so often say, 'Ah, that's a hard nut to crack!' and why nutcrackers are always so ugly."

The Mouse King

When the tea things had been cleared away that evening, Clara sat down by Uncle Drosselmeier. She looked up in his face with wide-open eyes and said, "I now know, dear Uncle, that Nutcracker is your nephew. You know that he is at war with his enemy, the Mouse King, the son of that horrid Mouseyrink. Why don't you help him, Uncle Drosselmeier?"

Uncle Drosselmeier lifted Clara onto his knee and said with a smile, "Yes, my dear child, the Mouse King is following Nutcracker and will kill him if he can. But *I* cannot help him. You alone can save him."

That night, Clara was awakened by a strange noise. It sounded as if someone was rolling stones up and down the floor, and now and again she could hear a *squeak, squeak!* Then she saw—oh dreadful sight!— the Mouse King creeping through a hole in the wall. His eyes blazed like burning coals, and his crowns shone brightly in the moonlight. He sprang onto the table close to Clara's bed.

"*Queek, queek!* Give me your *SWEETS. Queek! queek!* Or I will bite *Nutcracker,* bite him with my sharp *TEETH. Queek! Queek!*" He then sprang away and disappeared down his hole.

Clara was quite pale the next morning and scarcely spoke a word. Often she was about to tell her mother, and then she thought to herself, "I expect they will all laugh at me and say that I have been dreaming again." It was clear that to save Nutcracker she would have to give up her sweets. So the next evening she took all that she had and laid them beside the cupboard. By morning the mice had eaten everything. But Clara did not mind one little bit, for she thought that she had saved Nutcracker.

But the next night she heard a squeaking again. The Mouse King was even more horrible than the night before! His eyes blazed like fiery furnaces, and he hissed fiercely, "Give me your sugar dolls, little girl, or I will bite your Nutcracker to death!" and then he sprang down and disappeared into his hole again.

Clara went to the cupboard the next morning and gazed with tears in her eyes at her sugar dolls. But when she thought of Mouse King's seven mouths, open wide and ready to swallow Nutcracker, Clara laid all her sugar dolls close by the cupboard.

But that night, Clara again heard the Mouse King's fierce squeaking. His seven mouths opened and shut—*snap, snap! snap, snap! snap, snap! snap!*—as he hissed in Clara's ear: "Ah *ha!* Ah *ha! Queek! Queek! Queek! LISTEN* while I speak. Give me all your picture books … your dolls and dresses too, the *best,* or you shall have no *rest.* Ah *ha!* Ah *ha!* Do as I tell you, or else … I will *BITE … Nutcracker … D E A D!*"

Nutcracker & Mouse King

Clara did not know what to do. She went to the cupboard. "Oh, dear Nutcracker, I am so unhappy! If I give up all my beautiful toys to the Mouse King, won't he ask me for more and more, so that at last I shall have nothing left at all? Then, in the end, he will bite me into pieces. Oh, dear!" she sobbed, "what shall I do?"

Suddenly Nutcracker began to move. Then his little mouth opened slowly, and he whispered, "Oh, dearest Miss Clara, how much I owe you! You must not give up your toys! Get me a new sword! a sword!…" Clara jumped for joy, for now she knew of a way to save Nutcracker. But where could she find a sword?

She ran to find Fritz and told him everything that had happened. When she finished, he said, "I have a general who is now too old to fight anymore, and does not need his sword, which is beautifully sharp." He searched the cupboard, found the general, took his sword, and fastened it to Nutcracker's side.

That night Clara could hardly sleep. It was nearly midnight when she heard a rustling and a rushing in the next room. All of a sudden there was a *queek! queek!*

"The Mouse King!" cried Clara, as she sprang out of bed. But then there was a silence. Finally there came a gentle knock, *rat tat! tat!* on the door. A tiny voice said, "Dearest Miss Clara, don't be afraid."

She recognized Nutcracker's voice and opened the door at once. When Nutcracker saw Clara he fell down on one knee and said, "Dearest lady, you alone gave me courage and strength to fight my enemy. The cowardly Mouse King now lies dead! Accept from me, your knight, these tokens of victory!" He held up the seven golden crowns to Clara, who accepted them with joy and delight.

Then Nutcracker spoke once more, "Dearest Miss Clara, follow me! Now that I have conquered my enemy, I can show you wonderful things."

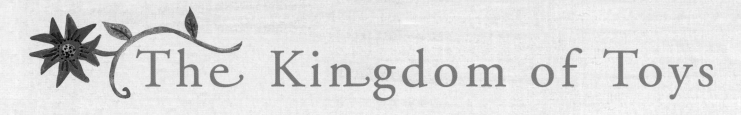

The Kingdom of Toys

Clara followed Nutcracker to the great wardrobe in the corner of the room. To her astonishment, the doors, which were usually closed, stood wide open. She could see Father's thick winter overcoat hanging in front. Nutcracker climbed up the coat until he reached the lowest button. He gave it a sharp pull, and a little flight of wooden steps unrolled itself down the sleeve.

"Please climb up, Miss Clara!" cried Nutcracker.

Clara had just got to the bottom of the sleeve and was looking over the cuff, when a blinding light shone over everything, and she found herself standing in a beautiful meadow with the most delightful flowers sparkling like jewels all round her.

They crossed the meadow and came to a forest of pine trees so high that Clara could scarcely see the tops of them, and so close together that when she looked into the forest it was just like peeping into a long dark tunnel. Then, suddenly, as if by magic, they were out in the beautiful sunshine once more.

Nutcracker clapped his hands and little shepherds and shepherdesses came running toward them. They were so finely made that you would have thought they were sugar figures. A shepherd played music upon his pipes and they began to dance.

Very soon there was a smell of roses in the air. The sky became a beautiful rose color. Little springs of rosewater splashed and gurgled. A big lake stretched on both sides with white swans in golden collars.

"Oh," cried Clara, "that is just the kind of lake Uncle Drosselmeier was going to make for me."

Nutcracker laughed. "Your Uncle could *never* make a lake like that. But never mind; let us cross the lake to the capital."

Nutcracker's Land

Clara saw a ship drawn by two golden dolphins sailing toward them. Nine little boys dressed in coats and caps made of canary feathers sprang onto the shore and carried Clara and Nutcracker into the ship. It was lovely, so lovely, to be carried along like a princess in her carriage! The dolphins blew streams of crystal water high into the air, and as these fell in glittering showers it sounded as if silvery voices were singing.

Shortly they reached the shore of the capital. I can scarcely describe this wonderful city. The walls and towers were of the most brilliant colors, and the houses were built in all sorts of curious shapes. As they passed through the city gate, which looked as if it were made of macaroons and sugared fruits, silver soldiers presented arms. Next came the marketplace. In the middle stood a great cake, and at each of its four corners a fountain spouted lemonade. But the prettiest sight of all was the thousands and thousands of little people who laughed and sang. There were beautifully dressed gentlemen and ladies, officers and soldiers, shepherds, clowns—in fact, all the important people one finds in the world.

Farther on, Clara saw a castle with a hundred towers soaring high up into the air.

"That is Biscuit Castle," said Nutcracker.

The doors of the castle opened and three ladies stepped out. They were so splendidly and richly dressed that Clara knew they must be princesses. They embraced Nutcracker and exclaimed, "Welcome, Brother!"

Taking Clara by the hand, Nutcracker said, "This is Miss Clara, the young lady who saved my life. Did she not throw her slipper at the right moment? Did she not find a sword for me? If she had not, I should now be lying bitten to death by the wicked Mouse King."

The three princesses cried, "She saved the life of our beloved brother!" and embraced Clara tenderly. Then they led Nutcracker and Clara inside the castle and into a large room that had walls made of the brightest crystal. The princesses invited Clara and Nutcracker to take a seat. Royal Servers brought in a number of little cups and dishes, all made of the finest porcelain, with knives, forks, and spoons of gold and silver. Next they brought sweets, fruit, and plates of dainty treats.

Nutcracker began to tell them the story of his battle with the Mouse King. Gradually his voice seemed to grow fainter and fainter. Clara heard a curious humming, buzzing noise, and then she found herself floating up in the air, higher and higher, higher and higher, higher and higher….

How It All Ended

Bang! Clara fell down from *ever* such a height! When she opened her eyes she was lying in her bed; it was broad daylight, and Mother was standing beside her bed. Clara began to tell all about her wonderful journey. "Oh, Mother, Nutcracker has taken me to so many places, and I've seen such beautiful things!"

"Dear," said her mother, "you have had a splendid dream, but it's time to get up."

Just at that moment Uncle Drosselmeier arrived. Clara ran to him, crying, "Uncle, tell them that it wasn't a dream! Tell them that my Nutcracker is your nephew and that he gave me the seven crowns!"

Uncle Drosselmeier made a funny face and murmured, "Stuff and nonsense!"

Then Father took Clara on his knee and said, "Now, my dear little girl, you must forget all about these dreams." Although Clara could not talk to anyone about her wonderful journey, she visited it in her dreams, and often she would sit quite still with her hands in her lap thinking over all she had seen and heard.

One day Clara was looking at Nutcracker lying quietly on his shelf. She said, "Oh, dear Nutcracker, if you were once alive again I would not do as Princess Pirlipat did and give you up. No, I would *not* give you up, just because you were no longer handsome!"

At that moment there was a loud *bang!* and Clara was jerked from her chair. When she recovered, Mother said to her, "Fancy a big girl like you falling off her chair. See, here is Uncle Drosselmeier's nephew, who has come to pay us a visit."

Clara looked up, and there stood a young man. He wore a splendid red coat, trimmed with gold, and white silk stockings. At his side was a sword, its handle set with diamonds. And he had brought presents—for Fritz a splendid sword, and for Clara a necklace with seven little crowns! At the supper table he cracked nuts for everybody, no matter how hard they might be.

After supper young Drosselmeier, for that was his name, asked Clara to show him the toy cupboard in the next room. As soon as they were alone, he knelt on one knee and said, "Oh, my dearest Miss Clara, at your feet the grateful Nutcracker kneels. You said you would not treat me as badly as the Princess Pirlipat did. When I heard those sweet words from your lips I ceased to be an ugly Nutcracker and became what I was before. Oh, dearest, if you will marry me you shall reign with me in my castle, where I am now king!"

Clara answered softly, "Dear Nutcracker, you are a good, kind young man. I shall be very pleased to marry you."

And so after a time they were married. At their wedding two-and-twenty thousand guests, wearing their best clothes and pearls and diamonds, danced merrily. And Clara and Nutcracker drove away in a golden carriage drawn by silver horses.

I hear that Clara is now queen of the land of Christmas Trees, lives in Biscuit Castle, and is very happy indeed.